Torti Kitty
Proud of Myself

This book is dedicated to the three most important people in my life: Autumn, Zion and Phoenix. I love you my sweet furballs for infinity+infinity+infinity. Be proud of yourselves.

Love, Mommy

Torti Kitty was a happy girl.

1

She loved everything

in her kitty world...

3

Like her mother and father
and two baby brothers.
But, she always wanted
to look like the others.

5

🐾

Mommy said,

"Torti, you're the way you should be.

You're a beautiful kitty who's perfect

to me."

"But you guys are one color,

you're black or you're white.

And I'm all mixed up,

so something's not right."

"You, my sweet kitty, are the best of us all. Like all the seasons at once, summer, spring, winter, fall."

"But I want to look

like you or like dad."

"You look like us both

so you shouldn't be sad."

"Be proud of your coat
because it makes you, you.
And don't change a thing
whatever you do.
Whether you wore spots,
stripes or even pink fur,
I would still love you
just as you were."

17

"Don't you see it's what's inside that counts? That's what makes you purr and bounce."

"I can never ever be anybody else.
So I'll hold my head high and be
proud of myself."

Tortifacts:

Male Tortoiseshell cats are very rare.

They are said to be good luck.

CPSIA information can be obtained
at www.ICGtesting.com
Printed in the USA
LVHW07n1659300318
571783LV00008B/130/P